ORCA
YOUNG
READERS

TJ and the Sports Fanatic

Hazel Hutchins

D1509932

ORCA BOOK PUBLISHERS

Library and Archives Canada Cataloguing in Publication

Hutchins, H. J. (Hazel J.)
TJ and the sports fanatic / Hazel Hutchins.

(Orca young readers)
ISBN 1-55143-461-X

I. Title. II. Series.

PS8565.U826T34 2006   jC813'.54   C2006-901018-8

First published in the United States: 2006
Library of Congress Control Number: 2006922290

Summary: TJ Barnes doesn't usually play team sports,
but he learns a lot about football and even more about
his friend Seymour when they both join a football team.

Free teachers' guide available at www.orcabook.com

Orca Book Publishers gratefully acknowledges the support for its
publishing programs provided by the following agencies: the Government of
Canada through the Book Publishing Industry Development Program (BPIDP),
the Canada Council for the Arts, and the British Columbia Arts Council.

Cover design by Lynn O'Rourke
Cover & interior illustrations by Kyrsten Brooker

In Canada:	**In the United States:**
Orca Book Publishers	Orca Book Publishers
www.orcabook.com	www.orcabook.com
Box 5626 Stn.B	PO Box 468
Victoria, BC Canada	Custer, WA USA
V8R 6S4	98240-0468

09 08 07 06 • 6 5 4 3 2 1
Printed and bound in Canada
Printed on 100% recycled paper.
Processed chlorine-free using vegetable based inks.

Special thanks to my son Ben, who does all things in life with enthusiasm and determination, and to coach David Owen, who encouraged me to write this book, provided invaluable technical assistance, supplied an endless variety of football stories and always offered support and friendship.

Thank you also to Lawrence Grassi Middle School, Reed Barrett's grade five class and the Haney family. And to local football teams and players, thank you for many exciting hours of great football.

Those above get credit for the accurate parts of the story. Any errors are entirely my own.

Chapter 1

My name is TJ Barnes and I don't play team sports. I gave up on that kind of stuff back when I was a little kid and discovered how lousy I was at T-ball. That's why I was surprised when Gabe phoned me. Gabe plays every sport in the world.

"I'm helping Coach organize things," he said. "First practice is Saturday, 1:00 PM. Don't be late." And then he hung up.

"What coach?" I asked T-Rex and Alaska. "What practice?"

T-Rex and Alaska are my cats. They're one year old—lean, lanky and with super spring-power in their back legs. We'd just invented a new game called chase-the-crazy-light-spot.

1

Alaska liked to chase the light-spot across the carpet. T-Rex liked to chase it up the wall. He'd take a huge leap, climb the wall right to the ceiling and come flying down again. T-Rex is great at sports!

He'd just done a ceiling flip with a single twist when the doorbell rang, the door opened and my best friend, Seymour, walked in. Seymour doesn't wait for the doorbell to be answered at our house. My family is used to it.

"Saturday, 1:00 PM," he said. "Don't be late."

Now I knew where Gabe had gotten my name—Seymour had signed us up for something. Weird. Seymour doesn't play a lot of sports either.

"I don't play hockey," I said. Hockey is big around here.

"It's August," said Seymour. "Not too many people play hockey in August."

"I don't play baseball either," I said. "I flunked T-ball way back when I was six and a half."

"Can you flunk T-ball?" asked Seymour in amazement.

"I couldn't catch, hit, throw or run bases," I explained. "The coach yelled at me a lot."

Seymour nodded.

"It's not baseball," he said. "What's with the cats?"

T-Rex was staring at the carpet with an intensity that could burn holes. Alaska was peering around the corner.

"Watch this," I said.

I held my wristwatch to the window to reflect the morning sun. A spot of light shimmered on the carpet. T-Rex crouched. His bottom quivered with anticipation.

Zoom. I sent the light-spot flashing up the wall. Up sprang T-Rex. He did a three-pawed landing way up near the ceiling and a spectacular dismount—a huge double-twister this time.

"Wow!" laughed Seymour.

Seymour was so impressed I decided to forget about being peeved at him.

"Okay, I give up. What did you sign us up for?" I asked.

"Football," said Seymour. He said it as if it were the best idea in the world.

"Football!" This was ten times worse than I'd expected. "Football players are huge and mean and they have to be able to tackle, catch, throw, run and kick the ball from one end of the stadium to the other!"

Seymour looked worried. One eyebrow went up and one eyebrow went down, which is what happens when Seymour is thinking. The next moment, however, he settled his ideas—and his eyebrows—back into place.

"Doesn't matter," he said. "No one else around here knows that stuff either. This is the first year they've had a team for kids our age. It's the perfect time to join."

"But does it have to be football?" I asked. "Couldn't we find some other sport that's just starting?"

Seymour looked at the ceiling. He looked at the floor. He did something very odd, even for Seymour. He shrugged.

"No big deal," he said. "I'll go on my own. Can't hurt to try."

Actually, it could hurt *a lot* to try.

Football players are gigantic and they flatten each other at every opportunity.

I should have said *No.* I should have said *Not in a million years.* That shrug, however, had me worried. Seymour is my best friend and something strange was going on.

"I'll come just to see what it's like," I told him.

"Hurrah!" said Seymour, right back at full enthusiasm level again. The cats caught his energy and danced sideways across the carpet. They wanted to play but the sun had gone behind a cloud— no more crazy-light-spot.

I tossed a cat toy across the room. T-Rex and Alaska raced after it in a mad rush of furry legs and armpits. They bowled each other over, tumbled into the dining room and slid across the hardwood floor. Alaska came out on top with the toy in her mouth. T-Rex was hot on her heels. Seymour began to call the play-by-play, football style.

"She's at the fifty, she's at the thirty, she's at the twenty…"

Alaska jumped to the sofa and took a giant leap through the two big railing posts on the stairs.

"Touchdown!" cried Seymour, raising both hands in the air.

After Seymour had gone home, I heard Mom come in the back door with Gran.

"Seymour just left," I said. "He signed me up to play football."

Part of me was hoping Mom would shut down the whole idea—no time, no money. I'd heard a lot of that lately. Instead she was nodding.

"Seymour's mother came to the store to talk about it," she said. "We didn't have to go far to look into things. It's well organized. There are proper age and weight categories. We have to buy the shoes, but they supply the rest of the equipment. It's a good chance for you to get outside. You can run around and get rid of some stress."

What stress? It was summer holidays. I liked sleeping late and not going to school. I even liked helping out at our family hardware store—I stock the pet supplies and fill in wherever Mom and Dad need me. I'm too young for an official job, so it's just for a few hours at a time. My summer stress level was about minus three. Perfect.

"But I have to warn you, TJ," Mom continued, "I'm not good with contact sports. I may have to watch your games with my eyes closed."

Adults are crazy. How could she watch with her eyes closed? I might have to *play* with my eyes closed, but I decided not to think about it. I looked at Gran.

"Will you have to watch with your eyes closed?" I asked.

Gran, however, raised both hands in the air, just the way Seymour had done.

"Touchdown!"

Chapter 2

At the store the next day there were boxes stacked by the back door. Inside were shoes with knobby points on the bottom—football cleats.

"How did you know Seymour was going to sign us up?" I asked my dad. "Why did you get us so many shoes?"

Dad was sitting at the desk in the storeroom, surrounded by stacks of paper and staring at numbers on the computer screen.

"I didn't," he said without looking up. "Mr. G. ordered them for the team. He's loading them into his car for delivery. He's one of the coaches."

Now I knew why Mom didn't have to go far to find out about things. Mr. G.

is retired but he works part-time at our store to keep busy. He came through the back door.

"Hi, TJ," he said. "Grab a pair and try them on for size. I didn't know you were keen on football."

"I'm not. Seymour signed me up," I said.

"I didn't know Seymour was keen on football," corrected Mr. G.

"I don't know if he really is or not. Something pretty weird is going on," I explained.

"Let me get this straight," said Mr. G. "You're playing because Seymour's playing. Seymour's playing because something weird is going on."

I nodded.

Mr. G. looked serious. He doesn't usually look serious. I remembered my old T-Ball coach. He looked serious *all* the time. Oh no. Maybe coaching was some sort of disease that mutated normal, happy people into intensely serious people who yelled a lot.

"Let me tell you something, TJ," said

Mr. G., raising a finger in the air. "There is one, and only one, reason to play football. And that reason is..."

"Money," said a voice behind us.

Mr. G. and I turned. Dad's nose was close to the computer screen and he was scowling.

"Football players make lots of money. They don't have to worry about damaged stock and interest rates."

The next moment he swiveled around in his chair and ran his fingers through his hair.

"Sorry," he said. "Even I know that only a small percentage of players ever makes money at sports."

"A tiny percentage, a minuscule percentage," said Mr. G. "Money is definitely not a good reason to play. The only good reason to play is..."

He looked at me seriously again. Up went his finger. I could feel myself cringing. I hate it when coaches think sports are the center of the universe and talk as if all the words begin with capital letters. Responsibility. Leadership. Team Spirit.

Self-Confidence. Physical Fitness. How To Win. How To Lose. How To Listen To Endless Lectures. That's another reason I'd flunked T-ball. I hate lectures. They drive me nuts.

All of a sudden, however, the finger dropped and Mr. G. grinned.

"The only reason to play is to have fun."

He scooped up the last boxes and trotted out the back door.

"Have fun!" said Seymour. "How can I be the world's greatest football player with a coach who wants to have fun?"

It was evening and Seymour had shown up at my house with his backpack stuffed to overflowing. When Seymour doesn't know something, he doesn't forget about it the way most people do. He doesn't go around pretending he knows, either. Instead, he checks out books from the library and he searches on the Internet. I was going to ask him what he had found, but first I had to clear up the reason for his latest rant.

"Seymour," I said, "you don't really expect to be the world's greatest, do you? The chances of being the world's greatest anything are really, really small—even Mr. G. said so."

"I'm not sure Mr. G. should be coaching," said Seymour. "He's a million years old."

"He's not a million years old. And what's that got to do with anything? He's smart. He's the one who helped us figure out the shoplifting scam," I said.

That was a couple of months ago. Seymour had spotted a lady stealing from our store using a knitting bag with a tricky trapdoor. Mr. G. had connected her with a man trying to sell security systems. Talk about a couple of con artists.

"Yeah, you're right," said Seymour. "He's like your gran. He's smart and sneaky, even if he is a million years old."

Seymour opened his backpack.

"Hmmm...he still might need to update himself. Maybe I should lend him a couple of the books I found."

He dumped a mess of printouts and at least twelve books on the sofa. His backpack must have weighed a ton.

"You're this worried about our coach?" I asked.

"I'm worried about us," said Seymour. "You scared me when you talked about having to be big and fast and able to catch everything and leap tall buildings and all that other stuff to play football. I had to find out for sure."

He handed me a book. It was an encyclopedia of sports. It fell open at a nice peaceful page showing people rolling balls along the grass.

"No lawn bowling," said Seymour. "Turn to football."

I turned to football. Players were arranged on a football field. Even in miniature they looked like monster men. According to the weights and heights written on the side under *Player Profiles*, however, some were bigger than others.

"Look," said Seymour, pointing to the middle of the page where some mini-monsters were lined up across from each other. "Big quick guys in the middle of the line. Big fast guys on the ends of the line."

"Fast and quick are the same thing," I said.

"Not in football," said Seymour. "I've been reading."

He pointed to the players around the edge of the page.

"The guys here are smaller. They're the ones who have to be able to run like crazy. Most of them can catch too. But they don't have to be able to throw."

He pointed again.

"The only one that really has to be able to throw is the quarterback. He also has to be fast, tricky, run the game and be cool under pressure."

I could tell right away that Seymour wanted to be a quarterback.

"Seymour..." I began.

"Who knows what we can do until we try," he said. "Somebody has to be really good—otherwise there wouldn't be star players! I've got another book with ways to test sports stuff."

We tested something called explosive style.

We stood beside the wall, tucked our right hands behind our backs and reached up with our left hands to touch the wall as high as we could. We marked the spots. Next we crouched and jumped up. Hey! Just like T-Rex. Then we measured the distance between the standing mark and the jumping mark and multiplied it by our weight. Seymour could jump higher but I'm heavier, so we ended up about the same on the explosive test.

Then we tested our reaction times. We took turns holding a ruler upright, with the bottom tip between the other person's thumb and first finger, and then dropping it without warning. Seymour could catch the ruler almost as soon as it was dropped. His reaction time was way better than mine.

We took turns looking at a page that had a single line with a dot two-thirds of the way down it. At least that's what it looked like when you were reading the book the regular way. If you tilted the book until it was flat and then raised it to eye level—in other words, held it straight out from your nose—the single line appeared to morph into two lines.

Seymour saw an X. That meant he had good binocular vision, which is great for sports where balls get caught or kicked or hit.

I saw a V—lousy binocular vision. No wonder I was terrible at T-ball. I was sure I'd be lousy at catching a football too.

Cats are supposed to have pretty good binocular vision, so Seymour showed them the book. They weren't interested. Alaska rubbed her chin against it, marking it with her scent glands. T-Rex wanted to play. He gave three explosive hops across the carpet and leapt high up the wall to tackle the curtain cord.

"See how he lands?" asked Seymour. "One foot at a time to reduce momentum. That's in the book too. Maybe they'll teach us how to do that at practice—how to roll and fall and stuff."

I was still trying to figure out how the tiny players in the book could look so large.

Seymour was tired of lugging books, so he left half of them for me to look at but I didn't get a chance. The cats like to sleep on hard shiny surfaces almost as much as they like to sleep on soft ones. They flopped across the books, gave each other a good grooming and fell asleep.

Cat hair, saliva and scent gland stuff. I was glad Seymour would be the one taking the books back to the library.

Chapter 3

On Saturday, before practice, I worked at the store. Usually there are a lot of customers on Saturday and Dad helps in the front. This Saturday was slow, however, and he didn't come out of the back office until it was time for Mr. G. and me to leave for the playing field. We saw Seymour walking, and Mr. G. stopped the car to pick him up. There were still a few shoe boxes in the backseat. Seymour's brain fastened on them right away.

"Guess how many pairs of shoes a professional team goes through in a year," he said.

"A couple of hundred?" offered Mr. G.

"Two and a half *thousand*," said Seymour, "for grass and artificial turf and rain and snow and everything in between. I saw it on a website. They also go through seven thousand sticks of chewing gum."

Once Seymour begins doing research, all kinds of strange information comes spilling out of him.

A lot of people had already arrived at the field. There was a buzz of excitement in the air—the kind of buzz that's hard to resist, even for someone who flunked T-ball. Seymour was right. It was a good time to join. Kids who played hockey or baseball were milling around with kids who'd never played organized sports. No one had played football. No one knew quite what to expect. And then Amanda and Meg walked across the field toward us.

"Oh no!" said Seymour.

Amanda is nice, which makes it hard to hate her, but she beats Seymour at things without even meaning to. It drives him nuts at school. It was going to drive him completely bonkers if it started happening on the football field. Luckily, Amanda is pretty straightforward.

"Don't look at me like that," she said, walking right up to us. "My sport is swimming. Meg's the one who wants to play football."

Meg's a good athlete. She plays hockey with the girls' team *and* the boys' team. Seymour, however, was still looking at Amanda suspiciously.

"Okay, okay," said Amanda. "My swim coach is dropping by. She's super interested in sports medicine and training for all kinds of athletics. I learn things just by hanging out with her. I might even help, if she'll let me, but I'm *not* going to play football."

A tall guy with a clipboard blew the whistle and called us together. His name was Coach Billings and he was the head coach. He talked about dedication. He talked about determination. He talked about the rewards of playing football, team spirit, responsibility and why all kids should play the game. Yup—he had the coaching disease...at least, he had stage one of it.

Mr. G. was offensive coach. Coach Mac was defensive coach. Coach Winguard was special teams coach, which meant he helped us with things like kick returns and placekicks and punting. Some high school players were helping too. Apparently football needs a lot of coaches.

First we did warm-ups. Then we did stretches. Then we did crazy sideways crossover steps, the running high-step and short runs back and forth on the field. Coach Billings called them conditioning exercises and agility drills.

"Pretty good, eh?" panted Seymour, coming up behind me. "The practice, I mean. Just like the pros."

I thought it was more like gym class. I like gym class and running around. I decided to enjoy things while they lasted. The yelling would start soon enough.

The coaches divided us into smaller groups and taught us stances, blocking and tackling. I was surprised we were already learning real football moves, but it was okay because they were just at a beginners' level. We worked with a partner and walked through the moves in slow motion. The coaches called it doing fit-up drills. Coach Billings said we wouldn't actually hit each other until we got our pads and helmets.

Pads and helmets? I hadn't thought about pads and helmets. Was that what made the mini-monster guys in the book look so big?

There wasn't time to think about it. There was way more to learn than I'd thought. It was simple stuff like "keep your head up, your butt low, your weight forward," but it was hard to put it all together. I had brain overload even if it was my body that was supposed to be doing the work. One great big guy named Gibson was having the same problem.

"How can I stay low and keep my head up at the same time?" he kept asking. "It'd be way better if I just put my head down and rammed through."

"Not if you value your head," said Mr. G., "which I do even if you don't." He worked with Gibson until he got it right.

"Bend your knees!"

Yup, the yelling had started. Coach Billings was walking around the field bellowing. "All the leg muscles in the world won't do you any good if your legs are straight. Bend your knees!"

After that, the coaches taught us simple pass routes, and they began throwing out the ball for us to catch.

"Do your best," said Seymour. "They're pretending it's all just for fun, but they're really watching us."

"Why?" I asked.

"To see what positions they'll assign us. Who can run. Who can catch. Who gets to do the good stuff."

They didn't have to watch me for very long. I couldn't run as fast as Shimu, Gabe, Meg or Leroy. I can't catch and I didn't even try throwing because I knew how bad I was at that from T-ball. And when I went off to stand on the sidelines, Coach Billings bellowed at me.

"You on the sidelines! Ten push-ups if you've got nothing better to do."

That's the kind of thing my old T-ball coach used to do—single a kid out and yell at him. I could feel my face getting redder and redder. I wasn't six years old anymore. I didn't like being yelled at. I walked off the field.

Well, I turned to walk off the field, but I didn't actually get there. I bumped into Gibson and two other guys who'd also been standing on the sidelines. I guess the coach hadn't singled me out after all.

We looked at each other. It didn't seem so bad if Coach was yelling at all four of us.

One kid rolled his eyes. Another kid called out "Yes sir, Coach, sir!" as if we were in the army. I thought Coach Billings would go all red-faced and throw the kid off the field for being smart. He didn't. He simply bellowed again.

"Ten of the best!"

While we were counting our way through the push-ups, Gabe stopped nearby to tie a shoe that didn't need tying.

"Next time you feel like a break, don't just head off on your own," he said. "Mill around with the rest of the team."

Leroy walked past on his way to get a drink of water.

"You guys are such wimps," he said.

Leroy can be a real jerk. Gibson, however, just looked up and grinned.

"Ten!" called out Gibson, even though the push-up count was only at seven. He jumped to his feet and headed back onto the field. The rest of us followed.

We ended up in the line for passing drills. Or dropping drills in my case. Either way it meant more running. I was pretty much beat by the time Coach blew his whistle.

"Good practice!" he bellowed.

Except we weren't finished. It was time to run wind sprints. How could they make us run around like crazy when we were already exhausted?

After that, Coach Billings gave us the same lecture he'd started with, only in reverse order—responsibility, team spirit, rewards, determination, dedication.

Mr. G. walked over with a football. "Seymour, you're pretty fast on your feet, but I'm guessing you haven't played a lot of ball sports. Am I right?"

Seymour went into deep-think mode. One eyebrow went up and one eyebrow went down. Mr. G. looked at me for a translation. I had no idea what was going on in Seymour's head. When it came to football, things were definitely weird.

Mr. G. held out the ball. I knew it was time for the same line I'd heard when I was in T-ball—*Get your dad to throw you a few*. It had never worked for me because my dad doesn't play sports. It wasn't going to work with Seymour either, because Seymour lives with his mom. I guess Mr. G. knew that because he said things differently.

"Take this football home," said Mr. G. "Get used to handling it. Get someone to throw it to you—your mom, a neighbor, maybe TJ if you can talk him into it."

He turned to me.

"And TJ, I want you to remember something because I think you're going to need it."

"What?" I asked.

"A second is five yards," he said.

Before I could ask what he meant, he walked away.

Chapter 4

"It means we're both lousy football players, that's what it means," said Seymour as we walked back to my place.

I'd known I'd be lousy—why was I feeling down about it? And what had Mr. G. really meant by "a second is five yards"?

I looked at Seymour. He was feeling way worse than I was. He was practically dragging along the sidewalk. Talk about over-reacting. I was the one who was lousy at football, and he was the one acting like it was the end of the world.

"Come on, Seymour," I said. "At least Mr. G. thinks you'll be able to catch once you have a chance to practice. And you can actually run."

"Not as fast as I need to," said Seymour.

"Need to for what?" I asked. "This isn't the pros, for crying out loud. It doesn't matter!"

Seymour looked at the sky. He looked at the trees. He wasn't in his deep-think coma, but something was definitely churning around in his brain, and it was something I didn't understand at all. Without saying goodbye, he turned and walked away.

Seymour never just turns and walks away! He's not like that. But I'd had it with Seymour. I was tired. I was suffering from football overload. No way was I going to run after him.

Some people have a watchdog. I have my own personal watchcat, complete with TJ radar. Alaska spends most of her day asleep, but no matter what time I come home, she's always awake and watching out the window when I arrive.

Too bad I couldn't teach her to answer the phone because I could hear it ringing like crazy. I hurried to unlock the door, leapt over T-Rex as he rushed toward me, and got to the phone just before the answering machine cut in.

Mom was living up to her "worrywart" prediction when it came to football. "Are you still in one piece?" she asked.

"Yup," I said.

"Good," she said. "Is Seymour in one piece too?"

"Yup," I said, "except he's even weirder than usual."

Mom sighed.

"Try and be patient with him. It's family stuff, TJ."

I knew from the way she said it that Seymour's mom had told her something about Seymour and then sworn her to secrecy, or whatever moms do when they talk about things but don't want it blabbed around. Before I could try to pry it out of her, however, she went off on another track. "Which reminds me, your dad has a meeting at the bank today so we might be late. Could you throw the casserole in the oven? Oops, gotta run— a real live customer is headed my way.

31

They're an endangered species these days."

As I hung up I heard *thumpety-thump* noises down the hall. Before I could check on the cats, the phone rang again. This time it was Gran.

"How was football?" she asked. "Are the coaches still in one piece?"

Gran always has a different take on things.

"The head coach yelled himself hoarse," I said.

"Seems to go with the territory," said Gran. "Has the local paper been delivered over there yet?"

The only thing I'd tripped over on the way into the house had been T-Rex, so I knew it hadn't arrived.

"Not yet," I said.

"When it shows up, put it where your folks will see it," said Gran. "I'll phone them later."

What was that all about? I didn't have time to wonder. Something gray and black streaked through the kitchen followed by a long white streamer. Oh joy.

The cats were decorating the house with toilet paper.

It was everywhere—long streamers down the hall, fancy loops around the furniture. I'd only been on the phone a few minutes! I rolled the toilet paper back on the roll. It didn't fit very well. I knew why the cats had done it. They wanted to play.

Late afternoon sun is almost as good as morning sun for playing chase-the-crazy-light-spot. T-Rex had a great time jumping higher and higher. I was so busy watching him that I didn't see the mouse until it landed in my lap.

A mouse! It took me a second to realize it wasn't a real mouse. It was the fake-fur kind I'd brought from the store. Alaska was sitting on the carpet staring at me. Had she dropped it in my lap?

I threw the mouse down the hall. Alaska disappeared after it and I went back to playing light-spot with T-Rex.

Plop. The mouse appeared on the carpet in front of me this time. Alaska was sitting beside it.

I threw the mouse. Alaska brought it back. I threw the mouse again. Alaska brought it back again. While I was being amazed at Alaska, my brain was working away just beneath the surface. Pretty soon I'd figured things out.

If Seymour had family stuff going on, then there weren't a lot of possibilities. He didn't have brothers and sisters. His dad had died a long time ago. He'd never mentioned grandparents. Family stuff would have to mean his mom, and that probably meant it was boyfriend stuff.

Yuck! No wonder he didn't want to talk about it! Either the boyfriend was a sports nut who Seymour wanted to impress or he was a complete jerk who Seymour was trying to escape. Either way, the last thing he needed was to sit around moping about it.

I phoned Seymour.

"Guess what," I told him. "Alaska can fetch."

Seymour hung up on me. I could tell by the sound of the click that it meant we were friends again. I was right. Ten minutes later he walked in the door. The paper had arrived and he put it on the coffee table as he sat down.

"Cats don't fetch," he said.

I handed him the mouse.

"Throw it down the hall," I said.

Seymour threw. Alaska retrieved. Seymour grinned from ear to ear.

"Are you a dog?" he asked Alaska.

Alaska turned her butt on him, walked three feet away and sat down primly. She was definitely all cat.

Seymour played fetch with Alaska. I played light-spot with T-Rex.

"Look at the way T-Rex crouches before he jumps," I told Seymour. "It's like what Coach was yelling, the bit about bending our legs to have power."

"Plus his back legs are the size of turkey drumsticks," said Seymour. One eyebrow went up, one eyebrow went down. "Wait a minute! I don't know about cats, but I read about turkey drumsticks and sports— slow-twitch versus fast-twitch muscle fiber stuff. Do you still have the books?"

He found a diagram of muscles as if the skin had been peeled away. Gross but interesting.

I read over his shoulder. First the book explained it in turkey terms. Drumsticks are dark meat—lots of slow-twitch muscle fiber, good for running around all day. Wings are white meat—fast-twitch muscle fiber, good for flying out of danger with a quick burst of speed.

Then it explained it in people terms. Human legs have both kinds of muscle fiber. People born with a high percentage of slow-twitch muscle fiber in their legs are better at endurance sports and running long-distance races. People born with lots of fast-twitch muscle fiber are better at running short, fast sprints—like football players!

"Do you think they actually twitch?" I asked. I had a bizarre mental image of the illustrations in the book suddenly beginning to quiver. Seymour ignored me.

"Different people are born with different percentages. I can't do a lot to change the actual percentage," said Seymour, "but I'm sure I saw something about how to improve what I *do* have."

He flipped through the books again. When he didn't find what he was looking for, he stood up.

"See you later. Take care of the fetching cat."

After he left, I read more about different body types and different sports. The section about water sports really caught my eye. *Long-distance swimming is one of the few sports where the female body has a natural advantage over the male body...more buoyancy, less resistance, less bothered by the cold.* I would have kept reading but the cats started making a pathetic sound.

Meoooooooow.

It was feeding time at the zoo.

I filled their dishes with crunchies, put the casserole in the oven and made myself a gigantic snack. While I hunted for the TV remote, I accidentally knocked the newspaper off the coffee table. A bunch of advertising flyers fell out. A big new store that had been operating all spring was now having its "official grand opening."

Grand Opening Specials

*Super Spectacular Prices for
Home and Garden*

*Weekly Sale Specials on
Power Tools*

If that was what Gran wanted to tell Mom and Dad about, they probably wouldn't be interested. Mom and Dad don't buy a lot of stuff, especially if they can already get it through our store.

I shoved everything under the table. It was messy, but the cats would like it. Cats like to sit on newspapers almost as much as they like to sit on library books.

Chapter 5

Summer holidays are good for just drifting along. No need to think. No need to hassle. I tried to drift but it didn't work very well. Football reminders kept interrupting my drifting.

My body was one reminder. Every time I found a new part that was sore, I looked at the books Seymour had left at my house. Yup—an entire muscle group I'd never heard about before.

The second reminder was Mr. G. He kept asking if I'd figured out about a second being five yards. I had a few ideas, but I wasn't going to let on until I was sure.

And then there was Gran.

"Do you have your game schedule yet?" she asked. "Shall I come and watch you practice? How about watching a tape of a pro game with me? I know who won but I haven't actually watched it."

"I thought you liked science shows," I told her. "When did you start watching football?"

"One of my friends likes football. It's kind of addictive once you begin to follow a team."

Another reminder was when kids dropped by the store.

Shimu dropped by.

"I hope they put me in at wide receiver," he said.

Apparently Seymour wasn't the only one worrying about what position he'd play.

Gibson stopped by.

"Coach Billings is going to pop a tonsil if he keeps yelling across the field," he said.

I wasn't the only one who'd noticed.

Gabe stopped by.

"Uniforms are in. Some kids have already dropped out. We need *everyone* on Tuesday."

Just what I needed—the whole team-pressure thing.

Leroy stopped by.

"Your weird friend is running around like crazy in the park. I had a pet gerbil that died of a heart attack that way."

Trust Leroy to make a special trip into the store to tell me.

Amanda and her mom stopped by. Mom and Dad had gone to meet with the landlord, and it was just Mr. G. and me taking care of the place.

"I'll be back when your mom returns, TJ," said Mrs. Baker. "Are you staying, Amanda?"

Amanda nodded. Mrs. Baker left to run errands.

"Doesn't she like Mr. G. and me?" I asked Amanda.

"We're renovating," said Amanda. "Your mom's good with paint colors and ideas for blinds and carpets. What did you think of football practice?"

"Meg's already way better at football than I am," I said. "Do you know how humiliating that is?"

Amanda laughed.

"Her family likes contact sports," she said. "Meg's aunt plays rugby on the national women's team."

It didn't surprise me. And it reminded me of something.

"Swimming is your sport, right? Let me take a wild guess. One day you'd like to swim across Lake Ontario or the English Channel," I said.

Amanda looked puzzled. "How did you know that, TJ? I haven't told anyone."

I just shook my head. I don't think Amanda does it on purpose. She just naturally gravitates to things she can be really, really good at. I made a mental note to tell Seymour never to take up long-distance swimming.

Amanda stayed to talk while I restocked our pet supplies. A lot of customers must have been away on summer holidays because not much had sold. It only took me about ten minutes to fill and tidy the shelves. By then Mom and Dad were back. They didn't need me in the store any longer, so Amanda and I walked over to the park. Seymour was still there, running in short bursts like some kind of small crazed creature.

"Don't tell me," I said. "Fast-twitch muscle fibers."

"You got it," he panted. "And they've about twitched to exhaustion."

He flopped down on the grass. We sat beside him.

"Wouldn't it have been more interesting to jog along the river path like everyone else?" asked Amanda.

"That would be training for long-distance and endurance kind of stuff," said Seymour. "That's not what I need to work on, except any type of running helps the old cardio— you know—lungs and heart and stuff."

"Just don't start lifting weights," said Amanda. "My swim coach says lifting weights does more harm than good at this stage."

"Rats," Seymour said, frowning.

"But stretches are good after you've been working out," said Amanda.

They both began doing stretches, and pretty soon it became a contest to see who could wrap his leg around the back of his neck or who could tie her body in the best knot. Seymour was pretty good at it. When Amanda found out that he could stand on one leg and do some of the stretches, she was impressed.

"Flexibility and balance have got to help you somehow," she said.

Seymour shrugged.

"That stuff is easy for me," he said. "I just wish there was some way—besides cutting my leg open—to figure out what type of muscle fibers I have."

I looked at him in horror.

"Don't worry, I'm not dumb enough to do that," said Seymour.

"Genetic tests can tell, but that's elite athlete stuff," said Amanda. "And there are are all sorts of ways to be good at something."

"Right," said Seymour. He rummaged beneath some bushes and pulled out a football he'd stashed there. "Anyone want to throw me some passes?"

We tried, but neither of us were much help. Seymour and his muscle fibers headed home. I still wanted to know if they actually twitched. When I got home, I began to read again. I never did find out, but I discovered something else that surprised me.

Leg muscles aren't a person's strongest muscles. Jaw muscles are stronger. Heart muscles are stronger too—all that pumping away like crazy. In fact, if you're in great physical shape your heart will push more blood around with each *whoosh,* and that means it won't have to beat as often. There was a chart about it.

Average adult...70 heartbeats per minute (at rest)

Athletic adult...40 heartbeats per minute (at rest)

There were other heart rates as well.

Gray whale...8 beats per minute

For a body the size of a whale?

Elephant...25 beats per minute

How big was an elephant's heart?

Shrew...1200 beats per minute

That worked out to twenty heartbeats every second. Maybe Leroy's gerbil really had died of a heart attack!

I decided to figure out the resting heart rate for a cat. T-Rex was sleeping in a sunbeam. I gently rolled him on his back and put my head against his furry little tummy. He decided I was a new wrestling toy. He grabbed my head with his front claws and began to kick with his back feet. Ow!

I tried Alaska. She's a whole lot more passive. Too passive. I couldn't tell her heartbeat from her purring.

I went back to the books. I was tired of looking at pictures of the human body with the skin removed. I chose a book with pictures of kids in uniform. It wasn't about playing football, exactly; it was about coaching football. And it shed a whole new light on things.

Chapter 6

You feel really big when you put on your football pads and uniform. Big chest. Big shoulders. Big legs. I felt like I could tackle the world—once I learned to run with my legs padded. And then I put on my helmet and became Monster Man.

Everyone else felt that way too. Kids began bouncing off each other or slapping each other on the helmet. It felt good in a weird sort of way. Seymour grinned at me. Behind my face guard, I was grinning right back.

The dressing rooms at the park had been opened just for this afternoon. As kids finished suiting up you could see them sneak a peek over their shoulders into the cracked mirror above the sinks.

I snuck a peek myself. Yup, I looked like a football player. And this time, when I stepped onto the field, I *felt* like a football player.

It was all part of the secret plan.

Getting kids interested and keeping them interested—that was an entire section in the book I'd read. The sooner kids had team uniforms the better.

And Seymour was right about the coaches sizing us up to see what positions we'd play—more of the secret plan. Okay, it wasn't so secret if people wrote books about it, but it was still interesting to read about football from a coaching point of view. One chapter even gave names to different types of coaches— some bad, some good, some in-between.

On the bad side were Sloppy Joe, Don the Dictator, Mr. Sarcasm, Buddy Too-Friendly, Mr. Superstitious and Sid the Sulk. My old T-ball coach had been a mixture of all of them. Yuck. No wonder I hadn't liked T-ball!

On the better side were Football Fan, Statistical Simon, Arnie Organizer,

Mr. Calm and Cool, Professor Football and The Doc. I began to match our football coaches with the book's categories.

Coach Mac was Football Fan. He kept saying things like "good try—great effort." He worked hard at being supportive, but he didn't seem to know very much. It was Coach Billings who gave the real directions for the offense, with Coach Mac doing the follow-up. Coach Mac was learning, just like the rest of us.

Coach Billings was more complicated. He definitely had a big hunk of Don the Dictator in him, but part of him was simply Arnie Organizer. Right now he and Amanda's swim coach, Sandy, were checking someone's knee, so I added The Doc to Coach Billings' list. There were other parts that I felt could go either way.

I didn't get a chance to think about the other coaches because practice was starting.

This time Sandy was on the field to help run warm-ups, stretches and conditioning drills. She was smart and fun and didn't make you feel like an idiot when she told you training stuff. I could see why Amanda wanted to hang out with her.

After that, Coach Billings put us into groups to work with position coaches. He made it clear that nothing was final yet. Anyone who wanted to try out a different position was welcome to do so. I'd read the book, of course, and knew that in the end he would still be the one to decide—as Don the Dictator—but at least he was giving kids a chance to learn about other positions.

He called Gabe, Leroy and one other kid to learn quarterback skills. Right away, Seymour jogged over to join them.

He called Meg, Shimu and others to work on catching and running. They'd be the offensive backfield, for when we had the ball and were trying to score. The book had predicted that lots of players would want these positions. Sure enough, when Coach said anyone with half-decent running speed could join them, more kids trotted over.

Next, Coach Billings put together the defensive backfield, the players who'd try to protect our goal line when the other team had the ball. It was a small group because so many kids had joined the offensive side. That would change. More of the secret plan.

And that left the rest of us. The book had even described this moment. It was the moment when kids who'd dreamed of scoring touchdowns and being football heroes suddenly realized they'd be standing in the middle of the field pushing against each other. They would be the linemen. Disappointment— big-time.

Beside me, Gibson frowned. He was the biggest kid on the team and anyone could have guessed where he'd be playing, but he'd been thinking exactly the way the book had predicted. I knew how he felt. In some strange place deep inside me—even though I knew I ran slower than most kids and had a terrible time hanging onto the ball—I'd hoped to be a runner or receiver myself.

"Linemen are the unsung heroes," I said.

I didn't know if it was true, it was just something I'd read, but Gibson heard me.

"At least we can be unsung heroes on the scoring side," he said. He called across the field. "Hey, Coach. Put me on offense!"

"Offensive line—over with Gibson," bellowed Coach Billings. I followed Gibson. I liked the idea of standing next to someone big.

Whack. Oof. That's the sound you make when you start hitting. *Whack* is the sound of your pads. *Oof* is the sound of your breath. We weren't hitting each other; we were hitting blocking dummies.

When we did begin to work against each other, it was mostly fit-up drills again. Coach G. quietly repeated a simple mantra during the blocking drill: "Feet apart, helmet below helmet, hands inside hands." Pretty soon Coach Mac and Coach Billings were bellowing it. We switched to a tackling drill and Coach G. started another mantra: "Rip, rise and run." The other coaches picked it up too. That's when I decided which category Coach G. fell into...Professor Football. It was the teaching part of football that he liked.

We began to work on some of the plays we'd be running. Gibson had a question.

"Coach, once I've got the other guy flattened, I should watch for the ball, right?"

"Gibson," said Coach G., "the idea isn't to flatten your opponent, it's to control him. That's why it's called blocking instead of flattening."

"Yeah, but if I happen to flatten him, then I should be watching to grab the ball, right?"

Coach G. was still shaking his head. "If you touch the ball the referee will whistle it down. You're an offensive lineman. You open holes for the runners and protect the quarterback when he needs some time to throw."

"You mean I can't even *touch* the football?" asked Gibson in disbelief. "But there are interceptions! What if I get an interception?"

"Ahhh," said Professor Football, finally understanding where Gibson had been heading all along. "Good point. Except we're offense. We already have the ball."

The light dawned.

"I'd be intercepting against my own team," said Gibson. He turned and called across the field. "Hey, Coach. I'm switching to defense!"

Coach Mac welcomed him with open arms. I would have followed, but I didn't want to look like some kind of groupie. Besides, Coach G. had decided to try me at the right guard position and began explaining what that meant.

Learning an actual position was more complex than I thought it would be. I didn't have much time to see what Seymour was up to, but every once in a while I caught a glimpse of him. First he was working with the quarterbacks. Then he was working with the offensive backfield.

After break he worked with the defensive backfield. That's where he stayed.

We ended with wind sprints and the same final lecture. Coach Billings only had two lectures: one forward, one reverse. They both seemed to go on forever. The book needed another category—Longwinded Larry.

Coach G. handed out the playbooks at the end of practice. Playbooks are written in football code. They fall right into the secret plan idea. And in true Professor Football fashion, Coach G. couldn't resist adding to it when he reached Seymour and me.

"Here's something else for you to figure out." He took a pen from his pocket and wrote across the back of each of our playbooks.

$$F = ma$$

"He's gone bonkers from too much time in the sun," said Seymour on the way home. "Why would a defensive back need to know a math formula?"

It was hot and we were carrying our pads and helmets. Football players our age don't need to lift weights. They get lots of exercise lugging their gear around.

"Is that what position you're playing?" I asked. "Defensive back?"

Seymour nodded.

"Do you think a defensive back could ever get chosen to be a team captain?" he asked.

A couple of days earlier I would have thought he was being weird again. Now that I'd guessed about his mom having a boyfriend, however, I could figure it out. If he couldn't be a quarterback or an offensive player with a chance to score some touchdowns, at least he could impress his mom's boyfriend by being a team captain.

"Maybe," I said. "If someone's good at it."

Seymour headed home to study his playbook. I went home too, but for once Alaska wasn't waiting in the window. I understood as soon as I opened the door. The smell of shrimp had clogged her TJ radar. Dad was home and he was feeding the cats from a freshly opened tin.

Why was Dad home in the middle of the day?

He never did tell me. We just talked for a while, and then he went back to the store. It had been great to sit around and visit with him. A few minutes later, Mom phoned.

"Dad just left," I told her.

"Did you talk about anything special?" she asked.

"Yes," I said. "We discussed how weird it is that cats hate water but love shrimp even though shrimp live at the bottom of the ocean. It was a very deep subject."

Mom doesn't always appreciate my humor.

"Right," she sighed. "See you later."

I made a snack and opened my playbook. There were X's and O's and arrows everywhere. Too bad they hadn't supplied a secret decoder ring.

A page from TJ's playbook

QUICK SERIES

TAR 21 QUICK

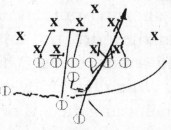

TAR 34 BLAST

TAR 48 SWEEP

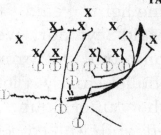

Chapter 7

"It's physics. F=ma is physics!" said Seymour, showing up just as I took the garbage to the curb the next morning. He'd found a new book—*The Science of Football.* "Which would you rather be hit by—something heavy or something light?"

"Something light," I said.

"Wrong!" said Seymour. "Well, not completely wrong, but half wrong. A bullet is light. A bullet can do a lot of damage when it's shot out of a gun."

He smiled and walked up the front steps and into my house.

"Okay," I said, following him. "But being hit by a freight train wouldn't exactly be wonderful either."

"Right," said Seymour. "Size *and* speed. It's physics—Newton's Second Law of Motion. F = ma. Force equals mass times acceleration. They even measure it in units called newtons for old Isaac Newton himself—gravity scientist and apple eater."

He plunked down the book. All kinds of formulas and definitions spilled across the pages—force, mass, acceleration, velocity, momentum, impulse.

"And it doesn't just apply to rockets and bullets. It applies to football. Small players can stop big players so long as the small player is traveling fast enough," explained Seymour. "F = ma."

He was right. That's what it meant. Of course, if there were big differences in size, then the small player would have to be traveling a lot faster than the large player. Either that or he'd need to hang on and get dragged along.

We had to do a lot of estimating and a lot of ignoring things like change of direction or how long a person could move at a certain rate of acceleration. But by substituting our weights and guessing that Seymour ran half as fast, and I ran a quarter as fast, as a professional team player, we came up with some figures.

Seymour had a force of 95 newtons.

I had a force of 54 newtons.

Gibson (who was big but sill almost as fast as Seymour) had a force of 125 newtons.

Good grief. Gibson could run right over me if he wanted to! Even Seymour shook his head.

"If I have to tackle someone the size of Gibson, I'll definitely have to hang on to him," he said.

There were pages and pages of football physics. Some of it was pretty interesting, like the fact that two big players who run into each other can experience nine times the force of gravity. It's only for a split second, but that's still a lot of G's!

The book also made a couple of important points. The first was that long before scientists thought of doing football physics, coaches and players had figured most of it out on their own.

The second was that physics couldn't allow for the "will to win" factor. The formulas were accurate, but things weren't always as predictable as they seemed on paper.

Still, it was fun to mess around with the figures. We'd just calculated that, at full speed, T-Rex had a force of 26 newtons, when Gran showed up.

"I brought the game I recorded," she said. "I hear you've got playbooks, so I figure this is good timing."

She was right. Both Seymour and I had begun to make sense of the X's and O's, which told all the players on the field how they should move to make the play work, but it would be neat to see if we could spot those kinds of movements in a real game.

Usually, when I watch a football game, I watch the ball. The TV camera follows the ball. That's not what I watched this time, however. This time I watched my position.

The right offensive guard on each team was a great big guy who set up on the line exactly the way I was supposed to when

I went into the set position. I could see him looking straight ahead at the players across from him. That's what he's supposed to do. He's not supposed to give away anything by angling his body to one side or the other. When the ball was hiked I could see him pushing forward to open a hole for a runner or blocking to give the quarterback time to throw. It really did work!

He wasn't always successful, of course, but even when the defense got past him, it was still interesting to watch.

I think Seymour was watching the defensive backs the same way. It was hard to tell because the tape had reminded him of the football web page he'd read earlier, and he started giving us all sorts of TV-type facts.

"That line across the field isn't really there, you know," he pointed out. "It's a virtual line to show where the first-down markers are on the sidelines. It takes a tractor-trailer rig of equipment, eight computers and at least four people to superimpose it on the TV screen."

"I thought it was added somehow," said Gran. "But why doesn't it draw stripes across the players when they cross it?"

"They have some way of adjusting it to allow for things like that," said Seymour. "Hey, look. Eye-vision camera."

At the top of the screen, a camera zipped along on a wire and was gone.

"There are about thirty of them all around the stadium and robotic platforms and all kinds of hardware and software and technical stuff to put everything together," said Seymour.

"Instant replays from every angle in the world," said Gran.

"Yup," said Seymour.

"Blitz!" Gran called out. The next instant, the quarterback looked like he was being swarmed. A few moments later, Gran made another call. "Screen pass!"

The announcer confirmed, "Six yards on a nice little screen pass."

"How did you know that?" I asked Gran.

"After a while you get to recognize plays even if you don't understand the details," said Gran.

"It's about people's brains being able to see patterns," said Seymour. "Some athletes are especially good at it. The best hockey players know where the puck will be three seconds before it gets there. Of course, they have to play a lot before that happens, something like ten thousand hours of practice."

Assuming that football would take about the same amount of practice as hockey, Seymour had 9,992 hours to go.

When Gran left, I realized I hadn't seen the cats all afternoon so I went looking for them. I found them in my closet, curled up in the middle of all the wonderful dirty-sock and dried-sweat smells of my practice uniform.

Oh great...I'd be the only player on the field covered in cat hair.

Chapter 8

For the next two weeks, we practiced almost every day. On weekdays it was late in the afternoon because most of the coaches had day jobs. On Saturdays it was two a day—practices on the field both morning and afternoon. Even at lunch we didn't have any time off. The coaches brought whiteboards onto the field and drew X's, O's and arrows to explain different plays, Sandy checked minor injuries and Amanda pushed the liquids at us. With all the gear players wear, dehydration is a big problem on a hot day.

It was a lot of practice, but Seymour said we needed it. His statistics were from a basketball study this time. A single move needs to be practiced at least two hundred thousand times before it becomes an automatic reflex. Why did every number he quoted have to be in the thousands? Or the hundreds of thousands?

Lugging the football gear back and forth wasn't a huge amount of fun, so pretty soon different people started giving us rides home after practice.

Sometimes we rode home with Mr. G. and talked about the differences between American and Canadian football or why teams with kids our age don't often try to kick field goals and conversions.

Sometimes we rode home with Meg's family and argued about football and rugby. Meg said rugby was better because there was more action. Seymour said football was better because there was more strategy and it was more intense.

On Saturday, Seymour's mom drove us home. She was alone, so maybe my second scenario was right. Maybe the boyfriend was someone Seymour didn't like, and he was playing football to keep out of the house and prove he was different. If that was the case, it was working. No boyfriend in sight.

It was also pretty clear Seymour's mom didn't know much about sports. When Meg and Seymour started talking about "zone vs. man-to-man coverage," she just kept shaking her head and saying, "I had no idea it was this complicated. I thought players just kicked or passed or whatever."

One day Dad showed up as we were finishing.

"I was just a few blocks away at the accountant's office," he said. "I thought it was a good chance to see what you're up to."

Mr. G. introduced him to the other coaches. They had a couple of laughs together. I hadn't heard Dad laugh much lately, and seeing him standing there with some half-bald guys with tanned heads made me realize that Dad didn't see a lot of sun with the amount of time he spent in the store these days.

We drove Seymour and Meg home first. After that we needed some groceries so we dropped by the supermarket near the highway. I'd taken off my shoulder pads, but I was still wearing the rest of my gear so I decided to stay in the car while Dad was inside.

As I was sitting there, I noticed the big new store across the parking lot. It was the one that had been advertising in the local paper. That had been at least a week earlier, but more sale banners were plastered across the windows. Apparently life was one big SALE at that place. Before I could see much else, a huge number 55 blocked my window.

"Hey, TJ!"

It was Gibson. He'd lost his practice jersey and was wearing his uniform, complete with number. I could tell by the look on his face that he wanted to talk about something.

"Are you looking forward to tomorrow's practice?" he asked.

The next day the coaches were going to run our offensive unit against our defensive unit. It would be a little like a real game, but we'd be playing against ourselves.

"I guess so—sure," I said. Gibson seemed even larger than usual. Maybe it was because I was sitting in the car or maybe he had actually grown a few inches. I was just glad he lined up on the other side of center from me. Except that's what he wanted to talk about.

"I think you should know," said Gibson. "Coach moved me to left tackle, but don't..."

"Gibson! Can you give me a hand? Quick!"

A woman was rolling a cart out of the new store with cartons stacked high.

"Uh-oh, Mom needs help. Gotta go."

Gibson took off just as the stack began to tumble. I didn't notice if he got there in time. You don't notice things like that when you've just gone into a state of deep shock.

Gibson at defensive left tackle! He'd be lining up directly across from me. I couldn't block Gibson. He'd flatten me!!

I phoned Seymour as soon as I got home. He agreed to come the next morning when I went to the store to talk to Mr. G. I even wrote out the physics on a scrap of paper so Mr. G. would believe me.

"125 newtons—that's twice as much force as I've got!" I showed him. "You've got to move me!"

Mr. G. laughed. The book doesn't even have a name for the kind of coach that laughs when you tell him something important!

"It's not funny," I said. "He'll destroy me!"

Mr. G. was shaking his head.

"$F = ma$. You're getting caught up on the m part—the mass. You've got to remember the other part—the acceleration, the speed."

"Gibson is faster *and* heavier than me!"

"Not that much faster," said Mr. G. "You're way off on your estimates, TJ. You're slower than Seymour and Gibson, but it's not anywhere near the "half as fast" figure you're using. Your comparison with a pro player is way too low as well.

And you've forgotten what I told you earlier. *A second is five yards*."

"But that's for runners," I objected. "If a runner gets a one-second head start, he can be five yards farther down the field than anyone else. That won't do me any good. I'm on the line!"

Mr. G. was being patient. I hate it when he goes deep into the Professor Football thing.

"It's more than simple distance," he said. "It's about reaction time."

"I've got an awful reaction time!" I told him.

We showed him the ruler test. When I dropped the ruler, Seymour caught it about a quarter of the way from the bottom, practically the moment it left my hand. When Seymour dropped the ruler, I was lucky if I caught it halfway along.

Mr. G. frowned. And then he frowned harder. And then his expression cleared and he smiled instead.

"Try it with a countdown," he said.

Now he wanted us to do a bunch of rocket experiments!

Mr. G. picked up the ruler and handed it to Seymour.

"Seymour may have a better reaction time in cold situations, when no one knows the timing. Football isn't like that. Offense *knows* when the ball is going to be hiked. You're offense, TJ. Your reaction time will be as good as Seymour's in this type of situation." He nodded at Seymour. "Drop it on 'two'."

We knew he wasn't actually going to say the number two, but that's how you call things in the huddle, and Mr. G. was deep into football mode. He did the quarterback cadence just as you would in a game.

"Down. Set. Hut. Hut."

Seymour dropped the ruler on the second *hut*. I caught it immediately, right at the lower tip. Even better than Seymour!

Of course we had to try it for Seymour. He caught it at the tip as well. We really did come out the same. Professor Football loved it.

"Offense knows when the ball will be hiked. Offense has about two-tenths of a second to build up momentum before defense can react. You'll be accelerating while Gibson will almost be standing still." Mr. G. began scribbling on the paper. "If we give Gibson an acceleration of one, then, using $F = ma$, all you need is an acceleration of one point three to equal him."

I looked at his scribbling. I didn't entirely believe it, but maybe, if I pulled out the "will to win," there was hope.

I told Gran about it when she dropped by the house just before practice. She was interested, but not as interested as I thought she'd be.

"How were things at the store?" she asked instead.

"Slow," I said. "Seymour and I had lots of time to talk things out with Mr. G."

Gran was looking at me in a strange way. "Don't you think that's a little odd? The way it's so slow around the store? I don't imagine you've gone through a lot of pet supplies lately."

"Nope. I've hardly had to order anything at all," I said. "Lots of people away on summer holidays."

"And yet the town seems pretty busy," said Gran.

"Yeah, I guess so," I said. "I haven't really thought about it."

Gran sighed.

"Maybe you should think about it when you have time," she said. "Just kind of be prepared for possibilities."

I was glad she said "when you have time" because I definitely couldn't think about it at the moment. It was time to head over to the field.

Chapter 9

The practice began with full team warm-ups and stretches.

After that, the defensive unit headed to one bench with Coach Mac, and the offensive unit headed to the other bench with Coach G. Coach Winguard would practice special teams on another day.

Coach Billings was the referee. He blew the whistle and it was time to do our stuff.

Gabe was our quarterback, and we went into a huddle, just like we'd do for a real game. We'd already talked with Coach G. about our first couple of plays, but it was Gabe's job to make sure we remembered, and if there were changes they'd come through Gabe.

The first play would be a running play. I wouldn't just be trying to stop Gibson; I'd be trying to push him aside so Leroy could run through the hole. I'd need all the physics I could get. In my head, I repeated my own mantra.

"Force equals mass times acceleration."

Down. Set.

"Mass times acceleration."

Hut. Hut. Hut.

On the third *hut* I was off the line and headed for Gibson as hard as I could go. Mr. G. was right. I had a split-second advantage and it made a huge difference. Gibson barely had time to take a half step forward before I hit him as hard as I could.

I bowled Gibson over! The whistle blew right away because our runner only managed two yards, but Gibson was sitting on the ground looking up at me.

It was his turn to be shocked. I helped him up. And then I saw something even more unexpected. Behind his face guard, I saw a look of pure joy spread across Gibson's face.

"Hey," he said. "This is going to be fun after all."

Gibson had been planning to take it easy on me! That's what he'd been trying to tell me the other day. We'd become friends and he'd been planning to take it easy on me. Now that he knew I could take it, however, he was going to *really* try to flatten me. He was looking forward to it!

On the next play he came at me about ten times harder. *Wham.* I held him, but just barely. And I didn't feel quite as friendly toward him as I had a few minutes before. In fact, by the time we'd run through five plays, I wasn't feeling very friendly toward any of the players on our own defense. I was seeing everything in terms of "them" and "us."

"Are you sure this is good for team-building?" I asked Coach G. when we stopped to regroup.

"Even the pros have trouble with this part of it," he said. "Just remember you're actually helping each other. If you don't put up an honest challenge, you're not helping your teammates get better."

I went back on the field to help my teammate Gibson some more.

It was a tough practice. That was good. Saturday we'd take another step up the "learn to do by doing" ladder—a practice scrimmage against another team—and we now had some idea of how the plays would come together.

In honor of the occasion, Coach Billings gave his after-practice lecture both forward and backward. Good grief. I tried to listen but my brain kept veering off. It kept bringing up images of the big number 55 on Gibson's shirt.

Why would I keep seeing the number 55? Playing against Gibson, or even someone the size of Gibson, was no longer a terrifying thought. And then I realized that the number 55 was actually blocking my vision and I was trying to peer around it.

It was like being shifted back in time twenty-four hours. The big number 55 outside the car window and beyond it, across the parking lot, the huge new store with SALE banners all over the windows. SALE flyers in the newspapers. People going in and out of the store while things got quieter and quieter down at Barnes Hardware.

All of a sudden I felt sick inside. Gran had been trying to tell me something that I should have seen all along.

Chapter 10

"Is the hardware store in trouble?" I asked.

It was suppertime. I'd been going to wait until we finished, but I stared at the food on my plate and knew I couldn't eat, no matter how hungry I was. I had to know. Now.

Mom and Dad looked at each other without speaking. It wasn't a good sign.

"Are we going broke?" I asked. "Are we going to lose the store?"

It was my mom who answered.

"We didn't know how to tell you. We..."

The sound of my voice surprised me. The words just came flying out.

"You should have told me. I'm part of this family too. I work at the store!"

"It's hard on everyone, TJ," said Mom quietly. "And yelling isn't going to help."

Which took away the mad feeling and just left the rotten sick feeling.

"Then it's true?" I asked. "We're going to lose it?"

This time it was Dad who answered.

"The truth is that we're not losing it," he said. "We're giving it up."

I couldn't believe what he was saying.

"But you can't just give it up! You've both always wanted to run your own store. You've worked really hard. You can't give up just because some big new place takes away a little business."

"It's more than a little business," said Mom. "I think you know that. Our store is practically empty these days."

"But people will get over the other place being new and gigantic," I said. "They'll come back to us."

Dad was nodding his head but he wasn't actually agreeing.

"Some of them will," he said, "but it won't be enough. This area is changing. The only smart thing to do is to close our store now before we lose a lot more money and a lot more time and still have to give it up down the road."

"You can't know that for sure," I said. "You can't see the future."

"We can't see the future but we can definitely see the present," said Dad. "We can't compete with their prices."

"Or their inventory," said Mom. "It's not just building supplies and tools. People go there for housewares, paint, window coverings, carpet..."

"Amanda's mother doesn't," I said.

Mom sighed.

"That's only because I've been giving her and some other customers a little personalized service," she said. "These days I have all the time in the world."

I turned to Dad. "At Christmas things were good. You could wait until Christmas to see what happens."

"The lease is up at the end of the month," said Dad. "We have to sign for three more years. The landlord is raising the rent."

I threw my hands in the air.

"How can he charge more money when we're making less?"

"Other people will pay what he's asking," said Mom. "And interest rates are going up at the bank."

Was the whole world ganging up on one little hardware store?

"TJ, there are things in life we can control, like how we run the store," said Dad in his most reasonable voice. "There are things we can't control, like how the landlord runs his end of the business or what interest rate the bank charges."

He said it so calmly that I understood. Beneath the surface he felt even worse than I did. He was doing the adult thing, but it was tearing him up inside.

I didn't want us to lose the store, but I didn't want him to feel so awful either. I did the only thing I could think of doing. I agreed with him.

"I guess you're right," I said. "I'm glad we talked about it. Maybe you and Mom can get jobs at the new store. You'll still be around hardware stuff the way you like, and you won't have to worry about money. It might even be a good thing."

Dad didn't reply directly.

"I'd appreciate it, TJ, if you'd keep this quiet for another week," he said instead. "We have to sign off on the lease a month ahead of time—that's next Thursday. It's best if word doesn't get around until then."

I don't think any of us ate much supper that night. Mostly we just pushed our food around our plates. After that I gathered a cat under each arm and went to my bedroom. I barricaded the door with my football gear. Me and the cats on one side. The rotten world of big stores, interest rates and landlords on the other.

When Seymour called, I only opened the door wide enough for Mom to pass me the phone. I wouldn't have answered at all if I'd known he was going to be on a rant.

"Their coach is an idiot."

Those were Seymour's words of greeting.

"You know the team we were supposed to practice against this Saturday?" he continued. "Their coach has changed his mind. He doesn't want a practice scrimmage. He wants a real game. Our team isn't ready for a real game. I can't be the world's greatest football player if the team isn't even ready!"

I didn't have a whole lot of patience with Seymour.

"Look, Seymour, why don't you stop trying to impress or un-impress your mom's boyfriend and just play the game?"

There was dead silence at the other end. Then a voice I barely recognized as Seymour's came across the line.

"What boyfriend?" the voice asked.

"I don't *know* what boyfriend," I told the voice. "I don't know that there even *is* a boyfriend. But it's the only reason I can think of for why you want to be the world's greatest football player."

There was another long pause.

"Okay," I said. "No boyfriend. It was just a wild guess. I'm not trying to make you mad."

"I'm not mad," said Seymour. His voice sounded normal...almost.

"So," I said. "Do you want to tell me what's really going on with the football stuff?"

I shouldn't have pushed my luck. When Seymour wants to talk, he yammers on at a mile a minute. But when he isn't ready to tell you something, he clams right up.

There was a small *click* and the line went dead. Not dead as in Seymour was on his way over. Just plain dead.

Chapter 11

When lousy stuff is happening in your life and you can't even talk to your best friend about it because he's acting weird, it's good to have something else to think about.

Football practices were longer over the next two days. On the field, all I had to think about was pass protection and blocking. After practice, Seymour and I kept it casual by talking football and hanging out with Amanda, Meg and the other kids.

The game was set for Saturday afternoon at two. Coach Billings added "game-day focus" and "football first" to his Friday lecture. I did what he told us to do. I went to bed at a decent time. I told myself to wake up ready for the game.

Saturday morning, however, it all went out the window. I woke up thinking about the store instead. I wanted to go down to the store, just like most Saturdays. Mom and Dad had said they'd be fine without me, but that's where I went.

Mom was with the only two customers in the place. I wandered up and down the aisles. We'd had the store for three years and I hadn't even liked it at first. Now, however, I couldn't imagine life without it.

I remembered the day I'd been put in charge of the pet supplies. I remembered the day Seymour had raced around waving fly swatters and talking about how they were invented. I remembered the day we'd caught the shoplifters.

"TJ, could you call me if anyone comes to the till?" Mom had scraps of material, pieces of carpet and cards with paint colors in her hands. "I can spread things out better for the Armsteads in the back."

"Sure," I said and hopped onto the counter. It wasn't usually allowed, but what did it matter now?

Dad had gotten tired of staring at the computer screen and watching the business go down the tube. He was out helping Amanda's mom hang her new blinds. When he came back I was still sitting on the counter.

"The Baker place is looking great," he said. "Your mom has real flair for choosing what works in people's houses."

"Some newbies are in the back picking her brain," I said.

Dad looked over his shoulder, thought a moment and then looked at me.

"I'm surprised you're so calm, TJ. Aren't you nervous about your first game?"

I hadn't been. I'd set football aside for the morning. Now that I realized it was almost time to leave for the field, however, my hands had gone cold and sweaty all at once. I felt like I was going to barf.

"Does your body make you feel weird when you're nervous?" I asked.

"Yup," said Dad.

"I'm nervous," I said.

Why was I nervous? I didn't need to be the world's greatest football player. All

I needed to do was hold up my end of things.

And that's why I was nervous. I *wanted* to hold up my end of things. I hadn't expected to feel this way but I did.

Mom came out of the back with the Armsteads. She waved at us. Dad and I headed out the door.

"I'll be back with Gran to watch the first half," said Dad as he dropped me off. "Your mom will be here for the second half. Hey—a positive side to things. When the business gets sorted out, all three of us should be able to come to your games together."

I knew he wasn't feeling as cheerful as he sounded, but at least he cared enough to try to put a good spin on the football part. He drove away. I turned toward the field.

Players in green and gold uniforms were gathering around the far benches. The only people not wearing football numbers were either coaches, who were moving about with clipboards in hand, or Sandy and Amanda, who were taping ankles for some players to help prevent injuries. I took a deep breath and headed for the green and gold.

The buzz before a first practice is nothing compared to the buzz before a game. Kids were way more excited and way more nervous. The coaches weren't a whole lot better.

Coach Mac kept up a running pep talk of "Great day for football" and "Are you ready there, sport?"

Coach Winguard was wearing one blue sock and one red sock and he growled at anyone who mentioned it.

Coach G. started quoting Shakespeare. "Once more unto the breach..." We only knew it was Shakespeare because he told us it was. Why on earth would a football coach quote Shakespeare?

Coach Billings got very, very quiet. Like an incoming storm. I didn't want to think about it.

It was a relief when we started to do warm-ups and stretches. *Just like a practice*, I told myself. *Just like a practice.*

And that's the mode I fell into. I settled

my nerves by pretending this wasn't a real game after all.

We had our lecture on the sidelines—just like practice. We knew what our starting plays would be—just like practice. All sorts of other things were going on, like referees striding here and there, people on the sidelines, a whole other team making noise on the other side of the field, a coin toss, special teams on the field for kickoff...but I kind of ignored all that.

"Offense! On the field!"

I snapped up my chin strap and trotted onto the field. We went into a huddle and Gabe called the play. We lined up. I even looked across at big Number 55—hey! just like in practice. The ball was snapped and...

Whoosh—Number 55 went flying by me. This wasn't anything like practice!

He didn't even try to hit me; he just headed for Gabe. Gabe handed off to Leroy, but in about half a second it was all over. Leroy was tackled. Whistle blown. Loss of yards. Huddle.

I couldn't believe how quickly it had all happened. Things were moving about twenty times faster than at practice! I needed something else and I needed it fast.

I decided to concentrate on the physics. Force equals mass times acceleration. A second is five yards. Offense has a two-tenths of a second jump on defense.

Down. Set. Hut.

Whoosh—big Number 55 went flying by again. This wasn't supposed to happen!

The whistle blew again. I forgot about pretending this was a practice. I forgot about physics. I decided to do what I'd told Seymour to do—just play the game. Play my position. Only this time I was determined that I was going to play it right.

Down.

Behind his face mask, Number 55 was grinning at me.

Set.

I made myself grin back at him.

Hut. Hut.

Wham.

I made the block. I made it and I held it and no matter what else was going on, I held it until the whistle blew. All of a sudden I was in the game.

In the game. Seconds passed in flurries as I pushed ahead to open a hole for a runner, or they stretched long and dangerously elastic as I waited in eager anticipation for the snap. Even distances seemed to shift as I rotated on and off the field with the defense, the game as small and close as the space separating me from Number 55, and as broad as the grass from one end of the field to the other. Everywhere and all around, things were happening and I was part of it.

It was exhilarating and—Coach G. was right!—it was just plain fun.

Except we got creamed.

Of course there were a few things that went right. Meg made a terrific catch. Leroy made a great long-yardage run. Shimu broke through the other team's line and sacked their quarterback. We didn't make any points, but at least we had some plays that worked.

And then, with our defensive unit on the field again, something unusual happened.

Thirty seconds left in the game and the other team had the ball. They were way ahead of us and were just kind of using us for practice—a cat toying with a mouse—which meant that the quarterback was calling a lot of pass plays. He called one too many.

Gibson saw the quarterback dropping back. He read the play. He raised his hands to block the pass. The ball was tipped to Shimu, who tried so hard to hold on to it that it went shooting out of his hands and—without touching the ground—into a third player's stomach. Seymour's stomach.

Seymour wasn't even supposed to be in that part of the field! He'd gotten confused and was way out of position. He'd been running forward and back, trying to figure out where he should be, but now he had an interception! He hung on. He started to run.

He was at the forty, he was at the thirty.

"Nooooooo!" shouted Gabe from beside me on the sidelines.

I looked at Gabe. I looked back at Seymour. I figured it out. Seymour was running the wrong way!

One of our own players began running after him, shouting like crazy.

"Stop! Stop!"

Either Seymour didn't hear or he thought it was encouragement.

He was at the twenty, he was at the ten.

At the three-yard line our player tackled him, but Seymour was determined and dragged our player with him into the end zone. Our end zone. The referee's arms flew into the air to signal a touchdown.

A touchdown in our own end zone?

Now even the officials were confused. They had to go into a huddle of their own. When they emerged they gave what Mr. G. agreed was the correct call. Our side would be "conceding" a two-point safety.

Seymour had made the first points of his career by scoring against his very own team.

Chapter 12

The way you feel when you lose a game forty-two to zero is awful. Horrible, rotten, worthless, low-level, miserable and depressingly awful.

You don't let it show on the field—you shake hands with the other team and say *good game*.

You try not to let it show when Coach gathers the players together for his little post-game talk.

You probably show it more than you mean to when your gran and mom smile and say *good try*, but they're your family so they pretend they don't notice.

And then you go home and barricade yourself in the bedroom. At least that's what I did—me and the cats on one side, the rotten world of not enough experience and teams that are better on the other.

When Mom knocked on the door to say I had a call, I only opened it wide enough to let her hand me the phone. I didn't feel like talking, but I figured Seymour was even more depressed than I was.

It wasn't Seymour. It was Gibson.

"I hate losing," he said.

"Ditto," I agreed with him. "Losing stinks."

"Coach Billings probably hates us," said Gibson.

I thought about it. What I came up with surprised me.

"Nah, I don't think so," I said. "I'm pretty sure Coach doesn't like losing, but I think he knows how to live with it."

When a coach hates losing to the point that he hates the kids too, he punishes them. He calls it something else—a learning experience—but it's not. I know because that's what my old T-ball coach had done when we lost a game. He'd yelled at us and then made us run laps as punishment, even when parents were still watching on the sidelines. No kid should *ever* be punished for losing a game.

All Coach Billings had done was give his same boring talk—he hadn't even yelled at us. The way he'd gotten all quiet before the game had been some sort of "coach intensity," but it hadn't been storm clouds. Coach Billings went up about three grades on my coach scale—Don the Dictator, Arnie Organizer, The Doc, Longwinded Larry and—surprise, surprise—a smattering of Mr. Cool. Who would have guessed?

Gibson and I talked for a bit and then I went back to staring at the ceiling. The cats fell asleep on top of me. When the phone rang again they made themselves heavier and gave me dirty looks. I had to slide sideways on the bed to reach the phone under penalty of death if I disturbed them. This time it was Gabe.

"I'm phoning to tell the O-line guys I appreciated the effort out there today."

Gabe was a way better athlete than I was, and he was a natural leader. But that didn't mean he could fool me.

"I thought Coach Mac was in charge of the rah-rah stuff," I said.

Gabe laughed.

"Yeah, you're right. We were all pretty lousy. But we'll get better. Tell your friend Seymour that for me. And next time we'll actually give Coach Mac something to rah-rah about," he said.

The next person who phoned was Meg.

"Amanda said to call and find out if you're as miserable about losing as I am," said Meg. "She thinks it might make me feel better."

"I'm miserable," I told Meg. "Gibson's miserable. Gabe is so miserable he's giving pep talks."

"Hey," said Meg, "I feel better already."

Apparently I was the team "cheer-up" person.

I went back to staring at the ceiling. And then I phoned Seymour. He didn't answer until the thirty-fourth ring.

"I can't believe I ran the wrong way," he said.

"Even if you'd run the right way we wouldn't have won," I told him. "They were a zillion points ahead."

"It would have been a big deal," said Seymour. "Our first touchdown would have been a really big deal for the whole team."

"The fact that you made an interception was a big deal," I told him.

"I quit," said Seymour.

I tried to change his mind. I tried then and I tried again later that night over the phone. I tried by going over to his house on Sunday, but either he was out or he wouldn't answer the door.

Monday I went to football practice. There was an interesting optimism in the air. We wanted to get better. We'd lost miserably but here we all were, back at practice. All but Seymour.

"You've got to make him come back," I told Coach G.

Coach G. shook his head.

"No one should play football because

someone makes them," he said. "Or because they think they should play. Or because they think they'll get rich. Or to impress someone by playing. He should come back because he wants to. The only reason to play football is to have fun."

I worked hard at football practice that day. I liked being part of a team, even if we weren't very good yet. I liked working with Gabe, Shimu, Meg and Gibson. I could even put up with Leroy. But it would have been better if Seymour had been there.

I missed him at home too. When you don't have brothers and sisters, it's great to have a friend who rings once and then walks in the door. Even the cats seemed to be moping around. I read them interesting sports facts. Maybe I'd discover something that would help Seymour.

A running back reaches maximum acceleration in two seconds.

It is physiologically impossible to run at maximum speed for more than seven seconds.

No help. If Seymour ran the wrong way, all that didn't matter.

Olympic weight lifters can lift four times their own weight.

Olympic long jumpers can jump five times the length of their own body.

It wasn't going to help Seymour, but at least it was something to talk to him about...except...oh no! The next couple of facts ruined things completely.

*Ants can lift **fifty** times their own weight.*

*Fleas can jump **two hundred** times the length of their own bodies.*

Seymour should have been a bug.

Chapter 13

If someone ever invents a machine to go back in time or even just slow time down a bit, they'd make a billion dollars.

They'd make it at football games, where players who mess up on an important play would give anything to be able to do it over again.

They'd make it in the regular world, where dates and deadlines come closer and closer even when someone wishes as hard as he can that they wouldn't.

I didn't want Thursday to come, but I couldn't stop it. I excused myself from football practice for family reasons. It was the day Dad and Mom had to sign off on the lease. The store would still be ours for another month so we could run a closeout sale, but Thursday was the point of no return.

Dad went to the landlord's office alone this time. I stayed with Mom. A few customers came in to buy things. A sponge. Two door hinges. Nothing that was going to save the business. Mom and I hopped up on the counter and perched side by side.

The door opened and Gran came in.

"I thought I'd pop by for a quick hello," she said.

Mom brought her a stool to sit on.

"Perhaps I will stay for a while," said Gran. "Thank you."

The door opened and Mr. G. walked in.

"Coach Billings has everything under control. I left early," he said. He shifted the lawn display in the front window and sat on the ledge next to a plastic duck.

The door opened and Seymour walked in. I hadn't seen him for almost a week.

"Why aren't you at practice?" he asked me. "I may have quit the team, but I still ride by on my bike every day to check things out."

Seymour had been spying and I hadn't even noticed! I would have been mad, but I was pretty glad to see him. He took in our quiet little gathering.

"Why is everyone sitting around?" he asked.

"Long story," said Mom. "Grab a seat."

Seymour sat on our stock ladder.

The door opened and Dad walked in. He looked at Gran, Mr. G., the duck, Mom, me and Seymour.

And then he laughed.

"You look like a bunch of vultures waiting for something to die," he said.

My dad had gone crazy. This wasn't funny.

We didn't mean to look like vultures. We were trying to make him feel better. We were trying to make us all feel better.

"Okay," he said. "This is good. Supportive. But it's not over yet. I need to talk to Rita. TJ, you can come too."

I was being included in a business meeting! Dad, Mom and I went to the back. Mr. G., Gran and Seymour watched the front of the store.

It wasn't a long meeting. Dad wanted to explain a new last-minute possibility he'd discussed with the landlord. The landlord had liked Dad's plan and had agreed to an extension of time. Now it was Mom who needed to think about things. Mom didn't say yes, but she didn't say no either.

When we returned to the front, everyone was still sitting in the same spot, even the plastic duck. I left the adults to talk about it endlessly, the way I knew they would, and walked home with Seymour.

I had things to hash out with Seymour, but first I updated him about the new possibility for the store.

"Do you think your mom will agree?" he asked.

"She needs to talk to the accountant and the suppliers and some people around town..." I began.

"But do you think she'll go for it?" he asked.

"If she doesn't, Dad says he'll think up something else," I told Seymour. "He says he's going to keep thinking up new business ideas until he comes up with one they both feel is worth trying. He's the kind of dad that doesn't give up."

And the kind of dad that doesn't like working for other people, I thought. I'd accidentally reminded him of that the day I'd said he could work at the box store. That's when he'd decided to stop looking at the downside and start looking for possibilities—at least that's what he'd told me.

"My dad would have been that kind of dad," said Seymour.

And as soon as he said it, I began to understand. Well, understand isn't quite the right word. I get to see my dad every day. Who knows what it's like for Seymour? But in all the time I'd known him, Seymour had never come right out and mentioned his dad before. Things had to be linked together.

I just kept walking. I didn't look at Seymour.

"Do you know very much about him? Do you know if he liked animals or cars or sports or anything? Did he like football?"

Out of the corner of my eye, I saw Seymour nod.

"He played it. I've got a picture of him in his uniform." Seymour wasn't looking at me either, but he kept talking. "Why should it matter? I hardly remember my dad. I just remember little bits like fooling around with a ball in a park somewhere. I don't even know if he's the main reason why I want to play or just one of the reasons. Do *you* always know why you do things?"

Let's see…I'd fooled myself into believing things were fine at the store until Gran began to drop hints. I'd fooled myself into thinking I hated team sports when I'd actually hated a single T-ball coach.

"I don't know why I do things *most* of the time," I said.

"Me neither," said Seymour. "Let's go to my house."

I'd already seen the picture of Seymour's dad on their bookcase, but that wasn't the one he showed me. The picture he showed me was a newspaper clipping—

a light-haired man with big ears and a bigger grin. The caption beneath it read *Local Football Captain Honored.*

"I mean, he wasn't a star or anything on a big-league team," said Seymour.

"But he must have been pretty good to be captain," I said.

"That's what I figure," said Seymour.

I tried to think of something else to say. "Is that the team uniform? I guess they didn't have all the padding and stuff back in the old days."

"I guess not," said Seymour.

"Who did he play for?" I asked. "Was it around here?"

Seymour shook his head. "It was in England. That's where my dad grew up. He met Mom when he came over here to work and he never went back. Mom's not very interested in England, but I'm going to go there some day."

Football. England. Something began buzzing around in my head, something I'd noticed in one of the books; something I'd noticed on TV too. Didn't Seymour know? Hadn't his mother told him? When she'd driven us home she'd said sports were a complete mystery to her, and she'd been confused about passing and kicking the ball around the field. Good grief—perhaps she honestly didn't know enough to realize the difference herself!

"I've got some cousins in England," Seymour was saying. "I'd like to meet them. I could talk football with them if I ever learn to play properly."

He definitely didn't know!

"Maybe they would take me to a football game where my dad played," said Seymour.

There wasn't any way around it. I had to tell him.

"Seymour," I said, "it would be neat, really neat, to meet your cousins and see where your dad played. But just so you know...it wouldn't be our kind of football."

"Different rules I guess." Seymour nodded. "There'd be a few different rules just like there are in American and Canadian football."

"There'll be more than a few differ-ent rules," I said. "There'll be a different ball. A round ball with black and white patches on it."

He looked at me.

"Why would there be a soccer ball?" he asked.

"Because in England and most other places, that's what football is."

"No it's not," said Seymour.

"Yes it is," I said. I thought again about the newspaper photo. I knew I was right. No shoulder pads. It was a soccer jersey. I'd even seen the explanation in the sports books. One of the names in England was Association Football, and the "soc" part of Association became soccer, which is the name we use over here. "I'm telling the truth. Honest."

"Football is soccer?" asked Seymour.

"Or soccer is football. Depending how you think about it," I said.

His eyes grew very, very wide. All of a sudden the full implication was sinking in.

"You mean I've been trying to play the wrong sport?" he asked.

But my brain had leapt over the down-side of things and moved on to the pos-sibilities.

"Maybe not the wrong sport," I said. "Maybe just the wrong position. We need to talk to Mr. G."

Chapter 14

On a crisp fall afternoon, Dad climbed a ladder at the front of our store and removed the sign that read *Barnes Hardware*. A lot had happened with the business during the past six weeks. A lot had also happened with Seymour and with the football team.

At the top of the ladder Dad paused, just for a moment, then handed the sign down to Mom. She took it gently. She nodded at me. I handed a new sign up to Dad.

Rooms by Rita

Walls had gone up to divide the old store into several small stores. Our new space was one-third the original size. One-third the rent. One-third the cost of electricity, heating and taxes.

Inside, things had also changed. The latest painting techniques, wallpaper and window coverings were displayed in decorated nooks. Two beautiful oak tables were scattered with sample books and color swatches. Mom would help clients plan from start to finish and order what was needed. Dad and Mr. G. would do basic installations. More complicated jobs would be contracted out to workers Dad knew and trusted from running the hardware store.

"I think I'm going to like getting out and about more," said my dad, climbing down the ladder. "Maybe I should start loading the latest order."

"Dad!" I said.

I pointed to a third sign. It was on our front door, and at the moment it read *Closed*.

"Okay, football time," said Dad.

A new team can learn a lot of football in six weeks. We'd practiced hard. We'd had five more games and we'd played every game better than the last.

"Are you ready, TJ?" asked Mom as she and Dad gathered tools and loaded the ladder onto our work van.

Hmmm. Let's see. Clammy palms. The urge to barf. Yup, I was ready.

No matter how many games a person plays, there are always pre-game jitters. That doesn't mean you should pretend it's just a practice. It doesn't mean you should think about physics either. The way you use pre-game jitters is to get yourself to that perfect point where you're ready to spring into action from the opening whistle. This was a whistle that our whole team cared about. It was the last game of the season. We were out of the playoffs, but we wanted to end the season with hope. We wanted to go out with a win.

There were two little problems. We weren't exactly sure we *could* win because we'd never done it in any of the other six games to date. And the team we were playing was the team from the start of the season—the team that had beaten us forty-two to zero.

"It's an advantage," said Coach G. "They won't be allowing for the fact that you've improved way more than they have over these past weeks. Believe me, the element of surprise is on our side."

Meg believed him. On the first play of the game she went straight into high gear and ran a kick return the length of the field. Touchdown!

The first play of the game and we were ahead! We'd only been ahead once before in our entire career. We were all congratulating Meg like crazy. Amanda was cheering wildly from the trainers' area on the sidelines. And we were about to make things even better by bringing in our secret weapon.

His name was Seymour.

In our kind of football—and this part is the exact opposite of the rules for teams with older players, including the pro teams—when a team scores a touchdown it can make an extra two points by having someone kick a convert through the goal posts. Most teams our age don't manage to get those two points because they don't have anyone who can kick accurately. A lot of the time, in fact, teams don't even try. Instead, they try for the play that works far more often for them—running or passing the ball into the end zone—which only gives them one extra point.

But Seymour could kick. He had what was needed. Balance. Flexibility. And soccer experience.

"I was only four years old!" he kept telling Coach G.

Coach G. just laughed and shook his head. "I know these English football players. Your dad probably had you kicking the ball around from the time you could walk."

Seymour's mom said it was true, she'd just never figured out the whole soccer/football confusion. There are all sorts of places in North America where soccer is a big sport, but it hadn't quite made it to our area yet—another reason why Seymour was unique. And Coach Winguard, who was in charge of special teams, had taken Seymour to a kicking clinic in the city to get him on the right track. Seymour had taken to kicking with a natural ability and a desire to learn that was even greater than anyone expected.

Our secret weapon walked on the field and kicked a beautiful two-point convert. Yes!

Right away the other team scored back on us. Six points. But they didn't even try the two-point kick, and we stopped their single-point run cold. We were still two points ahead!

After that we settled down and played the game. We didn't score on them but we held them right through the first quarter. And right through the second quarter. Almost.

Just before halftime, they scored a touchdown.

Going off the field at halftime when the other team has just scored against you is a huge, gigantic, way-too-miserable-for-words downer. They'd even managed to run the convert across. In no time at all we'd gone from being a glorious two points ahead to being a miserable five points behind. All around me I could feel players' hopes deflating like air leaking out of about two dozen punctured bike tires.

This wasn't time to lose hope—the game was only half over! I'd read enough of Seymour's football books to know what we needed. We needed a top-notch, spirit-lifting, halftime pep talk. I had a feeling that Coach Billings would finally come up with a good one.

He gathered us at the far end of the field and launched into it—dedication, determination, responsibility, team spirit.

Oh no—it was the same speech he always gave. Coach Billings was the person who should have read Seymour's library books! There were some great halftime football talks in the books. We were getting the same old thing, and the other team was probably hearing something amazing and inspirational!

I glanced down the field. They weren't. Even a football field away I could read the body language. Their coach was ragging on them big-time. His hands were flailing. He was pointing at players and throwing his clipboard over his shoulder. I could tell a couple of kids felt like crawling off somewhere and never playing football ever again.

I decided I liked Coach Billings. He might not be Mr. Inspirational, but at least we weren't being made to feel like a bunch of losers.

And anyway, we had Gabe. Don't ask me how kids like that do it—I couldn't make it happen in a million years—but he cracked a joke and slapped a couple of helmets and next thing I knew we were bouncing back onto the field.

When we lined up this time I took my position with the feeling that I was ready to take on the world. I guess a bunch of other kids felt the same. Our offense and our defense both kept the pressure on, big-time. We didn't score, but neither did the other team. And finally, late in the fourth quarter, our defense backed the other team right up to their goal line.

Gibson broke through and tackled their running back in the end zone for a two-point safety. Yeah, Gibson!

We were still behind—but only by three points.

Time was running out. When Meg came up with the ball again on the kick return, everyone's hearts jumped. This time, however, the other team was instantly after her and she barely had time to scramble a few yards.

"Offense—on the field!"

I snapped my chin strap in place for what would probably be the last possession of the game, our last few chances to score.

We began to move the ball down the field toward the opponents' goal posts—good solid plays. We were getting there, but there was a huge problem. We were getting there too slowly. We didn't have time to do this yard by yard. Time was passing way too fast.

I looked at the time clock. Fifteen seconds! That's all the time we had left to score before the game would be over. We needed a big play. I looked at the sidelines. Yup, Coach was signaling in a play. Gabe was nodding.

We went into the huddle. I was expecting Gabe to call a long desperation pass called a "Hail Mary," where the quarterback throws high and far and everyone prays the receiver catches it. It didn't happen. Gabe called a screen pass.

A screen pass! That was the short little pass Gran had recognized on TV. It was okay for a few yards, but it wasn't going to get us a touchdown!

You don't question the quarterback, but I guess Gabe saw my look.

"Secret weapon," he said.

I understood. Coach Billings was still calm and cool. I was panicking that this might be our last play before the clock ran out, but Coach knew there was time for at least two more plays. A few more yards were all we needed to be in field goal range. Seymour could come in to try a three-point kick. It would be a long kick, but we'd still have a way better chance of making it work than a long pass. And the game would be a tie.

Down.

I dropped into position.

Set.

I looked across at Number 55. I noticed something. A slight angle to his body—pointing, that's what Coach G. called it in football talk, pointing to the inside gap and headed straight for the quarterback. I needed to warn Gabe and I also knew the football code to do it.

"Check!" I yelled over my shoulder.

I don't know how Gabe heard me over his cadence, but he did. He'd been going to pass the ball but he saw the danger from Number 55. He also saw a way to take advantage of it.

Hut. Hut. Hut.

I blocked Number 55 hard, sealing him to the left. Gabe circled behind me safely to the right and...

Yes, oh yes! Somehow Gabe had relayed the change of play to our backfield. Leroy knew what to do. He was furiously lead-blocking to open a running lane for Gabe. By the time the other team tackled Gabe, we'd gained an extra fifteen yards!

Seven seconds left on the clock and not just "pretty good" field goal position— *perfect* field goal position.

Coach called a time-out to give everyone a chance to get into position. I headed for the sidelines to make room for the special team players. Gibson gave me the high five as he passed, going the opposite direction. Gabe retrieved and positioned the tee.

And Seymour walked onto the field.

He did everything he was supposed to do. He measured out his approach steps. He swung his leg high to make sure all the kinks were out. He looked calm and professional.

Gibson was at center for the long snap. He sent the ball straight to Gabe's hands. Gabe caught it cleanly. He placed it on the tee. He pinned it with a single finger.

But as good as Gabe is, even he isn't perfect. The ball was supposed to be pinned upright. His finger slipped and he pinned it at a slant. We could see it from the sidelines.

Seymour was already in motion—he couldn't stop now.

Gabe knew it was wrong—but there was no way to adjust things.

Seymour did the best he could. He kicked the ball hard and he kicked it straight. But he couldn't get it high. The ball flew low and fast straight ahead.

Wham! It hit Gibson right in the backside.

Everyone looked around in surprise, especially Gibson. Where was the ball? They'd heard the contact—it should have been up in the air. But no one could see it.

All of a sudden I realized where it was. The ball had rebounded directly back to Seymour.

Not again! Seymour was some kind of ball magnet. He was standing there holding the ball.

I heard Gabe shout, "Run! Run!"

There was huge excitement in Gabe's voice. Of course there was. If Seymour ran it into their end zone, we wouldn't just get three points; we'd get six points for a touchdown. We wouldn't just tie—we'd win!

But Seymour didn't move. I knew what was wrong. He was scared of running the wrong way. He was thinking out there—one eyebrow up, one eyebrow down. No one could see it because of his helmet, but I knew that's what was happening. He was thinking things through. Deeply. This way is our goal. That way is their goal. It was a good thing the other team still hadn't figured out where the ball had gone or he'd have been dead meat.

"Run!" shouted Gabe, gesturing with his arms as if trying to drag Seymour along. "This way. This way!"

He was ready to lead-block and show the way, but Seymour still wasn't moving.

"Run!" shouted Coach Billings.

"Run!" shouted Coach Winguard.

"Run!" shouted Coach Mac.

"Run!" shouted Coach G.

"Run!" shouted the rest of us.

I don't know for sure, but maybe, deep inside, Seymour could hear someone with big ears and a bigger grin yelling it too.

"Run!"

Seymour ran.

My name is TJ Barnes and I play right guard on our local football team.

Yesterday, with the help of my friend Seymour, we won our very first game.

Gabe's Big Play

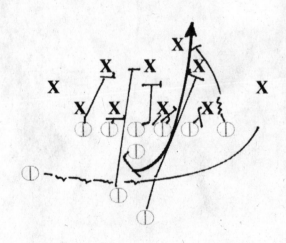

Some of the books and websites where Seymour and TJ found sports facts.

Books

Carol Gold and Hugh Westrup. *How Sport Works—An Ontario Science Centre Book*. Toronto: Kids Can Press, 1988.

Tom Flores and Bob O'Connor. *Youth League Football*. Chicago: Masters Press, 1993.

Francois Fortin. *Sports—The Complete Visual Reference*. Willowdale, Ontario: Firefly Books, 2000.

Tim Green. *The Dark Side of the Game: My Life in the NFL*. New York: Warner Books, 1999.

John P. McCarthy Jr. *The Parent's Guide to Coaching Football*. Cincinnati: Betterway Books, 1995.

Steve Parker. *How the Body Works*. New York: Reader's Digest, 1994.

Websites

http://entertainment.howstuffworks.com/physics-of-football.htm

http://electronics.howstuffworks.com/eyevision.htm

http://stuffo.howstuffworks.com/first-down-line.htm

http://people.howstuffworks.com/fb-equip1.htm

http://www.brianmac.demon.co.uk/muscle.htm

http://bodybuilding.com/fun/drobson33.htm

www.popwarner.com

http://espn.go.com/otl/athlete/monday.html

photo credit: Ted Hutchins

Hazel Hutchins has never been a sports fanatic, but she played basketball in junior high school, and she still remembers the single basket of her career. Everything she knows about football she's learned from her friend, who coaches football, from books and from watching other people, including her sports fanatic son and daughter. Hazel is the author of three previous Orca books about TJ. She lives in Canmore, Alberta.

Special thanks to Reed Barrett's grade five class, who helped me test some of the sports facts. Taylor Armstrong, Tyler Beringer, Douglas Bernauer, Michelle Betts, Timothy Breurkens, Hannah Brown, Ryley Chalmers, Miranda Chiniquay, Miller Denouden, Alexander Grant, Jane Gray, Jack Hayter, Justin Khuu, Kyle Lambert, Simon Newport, Simon Phip, Kentaro Plummer, Michael Stammers, Sean Stephenson, Marek Tannis, Hunter Turnball and others. My thanks to all!

Thank you also to Rocco Romano. And my appreciation to the Dinos, the Wolverines and their coaches for the enjoyment of watching their games.

Other books about
TJ, Seymour and the cats

TJ and the Cats

TJ and the Haunted House

TJ and the Rockets